It Tips

Written by Hatty Skinner

Collins

sit

sit

tins

pat it

pat pat

sit sit

tip tip

9

tap it

tap tap

sit in

it tips

After reading

Letters and Sounds: Phase 2

Word count: 20

Focus phonemes: /s/ /a/ /t/ /p/ /i/ /n/

Curriculum links: Understanding the world

Early learning goals: Reading: use phonic knowledge to decode regular words and read them aloud accurately

Developing fluency

- Read the title of the book to your child.
- Take turns to read a page aloud. Read the left-hand page and encourage your child to read the right-hand page.

Phonic practice

- On pages 4 and 5, point to and read the word **tins**. Ask your child to say **tip** too, encouraging them to sound out each letter t/i/n/s first, then blending.
- Repeat for the following:

  tips   sips   pips   pins

- Look at the "I spy sounds" pages (14 and 15). Point to the sandwich and say: I spy an /s/ in sandwich. Encourage your child to find other things that contain the /s/ sound. (e.g. *snails, slide, sun, scarf, skirt, sunglasses, candy floss, sit, octopus, snakes*)

Extending vocabulary

- On pages 2 and 3, ask your child to name as many things in the photo as they can. (e.g. *chain, woolly hat, red chair, lights, smile*)
- Repeat for pages 4 and 5. You could take turns to point and name the object. (e.g. *tin, tumble, dots, lines, patterns, boy*)